WARTS AND ALL

DREW FRIEDMAN AND JOSH ALAN FRIEDMAN

EDITED AND DESIGNED BY ART SPIEGELMAN, R. SIKORYAK, AND FRANCOISE MOULY

PENGUIN BOOKS

For Kathy with love from D.F.

*Special Thanks: Peggy Bennett; Pun'kin; Cheerio; Glenn Bray; Phil Felix,
who lettered the comic strips; and Dale Crain, for his design assistance.*

Also by Drew Friedman and Josh Alan Friedman:
Any Similarity to Persons Living or Dead is Purely Coincidental

Also by Josh Alan Friedman:
Tales of Times Square

PENGUIN BOOKS
Published by the Penguin Group
Viking Penguin, a division of Penguin Books USA Inc.,
375 Hudson Street, New York, New York 10014, U.S.A.
Penguin Books Ltd, 27 Wrights Lane,
London W8 5TZ, England
Penguin Books Australia Ltd, Ringwood,
Victoria, Australia
Penguin Books Canada Ltd, 2801 John Street,
Markham, Ontario, Canada L3R 1B4
Penguin Books (N.Z.) Ltd, 182-190 Wairau Road,
Auckland 10, New Zealand

Penguin Books Ltd, Registered Offices:
Harmondsworth, Middlesex, England

First published in Penguin Books 1990

10 9 8 7 6 5 4 3 2 1

Copyright © Drew Friedman and Josh Alan Friedman, 1990
Introduction copyright © Kurt Vonnegut, 1990
All rights reserved

Some of the selections in this book were previously published in *Bad News*, *Blab*,
Heavy Metal, *Magick Theatre*, *National Lampoon*, *Prime Cuts*, *Raw*, *Snarf Comics*,
Spy, *Twist*, *The Village Voice*, and *Weirdo*, and a number appeared as postcards.
"Sitcom characters in search of enlightenment" appeared on the cover of *Comic
Visions* by David Marc, published by Unwin Hyman.

ISBN 0 14 01.3086 1

CIP data available

Printed in the United States of America

INTRODUCTION

by Kurt Vonnegut

Many years ago now, for I am 67, there was a young bunch of American writers, mainly strangers to one another, who found themselves in a package which critics and academics found convenient. It was labeled "Black Humorists." Willy-nilly, I was one of those. I was living on Cape Cod at the time, and hadn't even read some of the others stuffed into that box with me. What we had in common, though, I came to realize, was a determination to show what foolish, misinformed playthings of good and bad luck even the grandest human beings are. What we felt we had to write made very poor propaganda not just for the United States of America but all humanity. We couldn't have picked a worse time, since humanity was then girding itself to colonize not just the rest of the Solar System but the whole blooming universe.

The best of our mordantly truthful successors, it seems to me, are much more effective than we were, particularly at a time when semi-literacy is epidemic, because they use troubling and interesting pictures as well as words. When I call them our successors, I only mean that they follow us in time. If they can be said to stand on anyone's shoulders, I would suggest Goya, and his *Los Desastres de la Guerra* and *Proverbios*. Can some of these people ever draw!

I myself have put pictures in some of my books, but I can't draw. A friend said one time, understanding what I had hoped to do with a picture, "My God, if you could only draw!" So I am overwhelmed by respect and envy whenever I come across anyone whose eyes and hand, when coupled with a brush or drawing instrument can make me think, "A picture really can be worth at least a thousand words." Thus did I come to know the name of Drew Friedman, whom to this day I have not met. I kept seeing his work and declaring that such draughtsmanship was clearly impossible. But there it was.

In my childhood, of course, I had seen comic strips which were drawn that well. *Prince Valiant* comes to mind, and *Terry and the Pirates*, and *The Saint*. But the words and intentions which came along with those remarkable pictures had no weight. It seems likely to me that humorless, uncritical boosters of the human race will dismiss the work of Drew Friedman and his brother Josh, his Ira Gershwin, and others like them, as being more trash for the funny papers.

Again I mention Goya.

Sitcom characters in search of enlightenment.

FRIEDMAN BROS.' NIGHTMARE GALLERY OF MENTALLY DISTURBED TEACHERS

MOST OF THE FRIEDMAN BROS' PUBLIC SCHOOL TEACHERS THROUGHOUT THE 1960'S WERE PROFOUNDLY DISTURBED INDIVIDUALS. YET THEY WERE THE MOLDERS OF YOUNG, IMPRESSIONABLE MINDS, LIKE THOSE OF JOSH AND DREW. HERE ARE BUT A FEW....

IN GRADE SCHOOL, MISS DOROTHY HICKS HAD TO BE PHYSICALLY RESTRAINED WHEN SHE SNAPPED DURING AN AUDITORIUM SCREENING THAT CONTAINED DANCING LEGS. THE MOVIE: SINGIN' IN THE RAIN.

OVER MY DEAD BODY, I WON'T LET THE KIDS VIEW SUCH FOULNESS!

MR. HALE WAS A HUMORLESS CLOSET HOMO, WITH DANDRUFF-BESPECKLED BLACK SUITS. HE WAS A CHAIN-SMOKING, 10-CUPS-OF-COFFEE-A-DAY, SHRIEKING, CHILD-HATING CIVIL SERVANT.

COACH YOHALEM GAVE THE SAME ANSWER TO ALL QUESTIONS.

HEY, COACH, HOW'D I DO?

TOMORRA, TOMORRA, ASK ME TOMORRA. SUNDAY AT THREE IN THE MORNING, ASK ME THEN.

DR. FLOYD PEABODY POTTS WAS ADAMANT ABOUT ONLY ONE THING IN LIFE.

YOUR MATH SHOULD TAKE PRECEDENCE OVER EVERYTHING ELSE. NO BASEBALL, NO HOBBIES, NO FRIENDS MUST EVER COME BEFORE IT.

Script: Josh Alan Friedman

There was only one way to deal with Potts.

BONK!

Jr. High social studies wacko Mr. Berkson spent the entire first semester studying something called "Umwelt." Nobody ever heard of it before or since, nor did they have the faintest notion of what it was.

Fathom the concept: UMWELT.

Wolfgang Chang, music teacher from Hawaii, forced students to perform "We're Going to a Hukilau" on ukeleles.

Can't we learn about Hendrix?

No. You already know about that. I want to expose you to earlier musics.

But classical music really, really sucks.

The only school-sanctioned "rock" lyrics involved the study of "Turn, Turn, Turn" and "Scarborough Fair." The teacher who taught English felt ferociously insecure.

Oh, dear God, why did you make my breasts smaller than mosquito bites?

MR. KNAPP WAS A ONE-MAN DRUG ENFORCEMENT AGENCY IN 1969. HE POPPED OUT OF LOCKERS TO STRANGLE PERPETRATORS UNTIL THE COPS ARRIVED.

HASH IS A NARCOTIC. YOU LITTLE PRICKS'LL GET TEN YEARS!

PRINCIPAL DR. BIXHORN REPEATED THE SAME MOTTO FOR YEARS.

MUTUAL RESPECT BETWEEN TEACHER AND STUDENT.

POOR MR. DISENBAUM BEGRUDGINGLY DEALT WITH CHANGING MALE ATTITUDES IN SHOP CLASS.

TUCK YOUR... HAIR, REMOVE JEWELRY, AND KEEP OBJECTS OUT OF THE WAY BEFORE YOU TURN ON THE JUICE.

TURN OFF THE JUICE!

BZZZZ

THE GENERAL SCHOOL POLICY WAS EPITOMIZED BY MR. JOHNSON, A SICKO ENGLISH TEACHER WHO GAVE DAILY PEP TALKS TO SELECT STUDENTS.

LISTEN CAREFULLY: YOU ARE A FAILURE. YOU HAVE NO CHANCE IN LIFE. YOU'RE SO HOPELESS, YOU NEEDN'T BOTHER TO TRY. YOU DESERVE STRAIGHT F'S....

GREAT NECK SOUTH

END

THE CARPET BAGGER

THREATENED BY POVERTY, HIS BAR MITZVAH FUNDS DEPLETED, MARNIN ROSENBERG EMERGED FROM HIS ROOM AT THE AGE OF 30 TO BEGIN A JOB-- CARPET STORE SALESMAN.

IMPATIENT RESIDENTS OF JAMAICA, QUEENS, CAME IN TO PICK THE CARPET OF THEIR DREAMS.

I'LL HAVE ME FI'TY YARDS OF THAT *FINE* YELLOW BUMBLE-BEE CARPET... MMM, LOOK *GOOD.*

HOW ARE YOU FIXED FOR CARPE[T]

I WANNA GET ME SOME O' THAT *MAG-NOL-EUM* FOR MAH BAFFROOM.

WHO?

THE JOB ALSO TOOK MARNIN INTO THE FIELD, INSTALLING ORDERS WITH HORACE.

AY- MEN, GLORY HALLE- LUJAH.

Script: Josh Alan Friedman

HORACE WAS A HARDWORKING JEHOVAH'S WITNESS, WHO SUPPORTED THREE KIDS ON $300 A WEEK AND NEVER COMPLAINED. HE COULD LAY CARPET LIKE JOHN HENRY LAID TRACK.

LIFE SURE IS SWEET.

SOMETIMES IF THEY ENCOUNTERED INFESTATIONS OF ROACHES AND GARBAGE, THEY'D WALK OFF THE JOB.

I AIN'T CLEANIN' THIS.

IF YA THINK I'M GONNA CLEAN IT YER CRAZY. I'M A WHITE JEW BOY.

MARNIN LEARNED HOW TO WIELD A TAPE MEASURE AND MAT KNIFE. THE TOUGH WORK CAME EASY TO HORACE, AWAITING PARADISE. HE REALLY BELIEVED THEY COULD RECARPET THE WORLD AND MAKE IT BETTER.

YOU SHOULD COME TO OUR WATCHTOWER MEETINGS. THE LORD SAVES THOSE WHO GIVE THEMSELVES TO JESUS. YOU NEED TO BE SAVED, MARTIN.

BUY RUGS NOT DRUGS

WITH CASH IN POCKET FOR THE FIRST TIME IN YEARS, MARNIN WAS INSTILLED WITH A NEW SENSE OF MANHOOD. BUT HIS PICKUP CHOPS REMAINED RUSTY.

LET'S BE HONEST. YOU HAVE CERTAIN NEEDS. I HAVE CERTAIN NEEDS. WHY NOT SATISFY THESE NEEDS TOGETHER?

IT SEEMED AS IF THE *JAPS* OF GREAT NECK CONSPIRED NOT TO PROVIDE MARNIN WITH SEX.

AS IF ALL GIRLS ON LONG ISLAND WERE INDOCTRINATED AT AN EARLY AGE NEVER TO GIVE HIM ANY.

THE ONLY PLACE HE CAME WITHIN REACHING DISTANCE WAS AT WORK.

UNDER NO CIRCUMSTANCES MUST ANY OF US PUT OUT FOR MARNIN ROSENBERG. LET HIM SUFFER, WITHER, AND DIE.

AND IF YOU *EVER* CROSS PATHS LATER IN LIFE WITH A "MARNIN ROSENBERG", MAKE SURE *YOU NEVER* HAVE SEX WITH HIM.

WANT SOME THEX?

SO MARNIN CHANNELED HIS FRUSTRATION INTO BECOMING THE GREATEST CARPET SALESMAN IN AMERICA.

BUT ALAS, SOME MEN ARE JUST NOT MEANT FOR WORK.

I QUIT. TAKE THE $20 IN THE REGISTER AND ALL THE CARPETS YOU WANT. I'M OUTTA HERE.

END

Penthouse publisher Bob Guccione fills up his water bed the ultraclassy, Perrier way.

MARNIN ROSENBERG IN
BAD LUCK WITH WOMEN

THURSDAY WAS "JAP" NIGHT IN GREAT NECK.

SAY, MARNIN, WHEN YA GOIN' ON *THE DATING GAME?* HAW!

AH, THE UNTOUCHABLES--HUNDREDS OF STRESSED-OUT PROFESSIONAL VIRGINS WHO PERPLEXED REGULARS LIKE MARNIN AND HIS PAL LARRY.

YEAH, IT'S BEEN TWO LONG WEEKS SINCE I'VE GOTTEN LAID... TWO WEEKS AS OF FIVE YEARS AGO.

CUCUMBER'S WAS INDEED AN ETHNIC BAR. THE JAPS HAD A TOUCH OF FANNY BRICE IN THEIR GENES. THEY WERE MARNIN'S NATURAL ENEMY.

MARNIN DECIDED TO STRAIGHTEN A FEW OUT.

WHY DON'T YOU ALL JUST *GROW UP*.... OH, FORGET IT....

TO CAP OFF THE EVENING, THE GIRL WHO HAD BROKEN MARNIN'S HEART AND DENIED HIM SEX DURING A BRIEF CALAMITOUS AFFAIR RAMMED HER TONGUE DOWN LARRY'S THROAT.

WARNING! WARNING! BRAIN DAMAGE, B-R-A-I-N DAMAGE!

WHAT THE !?

DYING INSIDE, HE HAD TO ESCAPE THE BARS AND FIND A WOMAN. FIRST HE TRIED THE PERSONALS.

AND WHAT DO YOU DO?

I'M UNEMPLOYED. I USED TO WORK AT A CARPET STORE IN QUEENS FOR A WHILE.

OH, UM... HEY, I'LL CALL YOU BACK SOMETIME.

I'M STILL GETTING OVER A PAINFUL BREAK-UP WITH MY BOYFRIEND. HE LOOKED EXACTLY LIKE MICK JAGGER.

IF VOMIT-FACE JUNKIE-HEADS TURN YOU ON, I'M NOT FOR YOU.

BUT THEN ONE DAY MARNIN GOT WIND OF A SERVICE THAT HE HOPED WOULD CHANGE HIS LIFE.

WE MET AT CASANOVA DATING. NOW I HAVE SEX ON A DAILY BASIS. WHY DON'T YOU TRY THERE?

WITH A LUMP IN HIS THROAT, MARNIN BOLDLY SET SAIL TO SEEK RELIEF FROM A LIFE OF INVOLUNTARY CELIBACY.

HELLO. I REALIZE THERE ARE AVERAGE-LOOKING GIRLS OUT THERE WITH GREAT PERSONALITIES, BUT WHY SHOULD I START WITH ONE? I WANT 9's OR 10's.

FEELINGS, NOTHING MORE THAN FEELINGS...

END
LONELI-
NESS
OVER-
NIGHT

THE POINT I'M TRYING TO MAKE IS, I WANT A GIRL WITH A GREAT PERSONALITY; BUT IF SHE'S NOT *VERY* ATTRACTIVE, SHE HASN'T GOT A CHANCE IN HELL WITH ME. SO I MIGHT AS WELL START WITH THE KNOCK-OUTS AND WEED OUT THE BAD PERSONALITIES FROM THERE.

I THINK WE HAVE JUST WHAT YOU'RE LOOKING FOR, MR. ROSENBERG. THE FEE'S $500 FOR A NINE-MONTH PERIOD, WITH A GUARANTEE OF SIX DATES PER MONTH.

MARNIN SHELLED OUT $300 IN RENT MONEY AS A DOWN PAYMENT.

JUST REMEMBER, I'M PAYIN' FOR 9'S AND 10'S. IF I DON'T GET 'EM, I WANT MY MONEY BACK. IT MAY SOUND CRUDE, BUT THAT'S ALL I CARE ABOUT.

ALAS, MARNIN WOULD HAVE ACCESS TO GIRLS BEYOND THE HOMETOWN HORIZON....WHILST AWAITING PROCESSING, MARNIN EXPOUNDED UPON GREAT NECK WOMANHOOD.

FUNNY HOW THEY ALWAYS ACT AS IF THEY SMELL USED KITTY LITTER. SOMETHING'S *ALWAYS* WRONG, AMISS.

THEY'RE MATERIALISTIC. YOU GOTTA LOOK MACHO, HAVE COKE, LOTSA MONEY, A REAL NICE CAR, BE AN EGOTISTICAL JERK. THEY LOVE THAT.

YOU CAN'T SELL A CAR TO A JEW OR AN ITALIAN -- THEY'LL EAT YOUR HEART OUT. MY LOT SELLS ONLY TO NIGGERS. THEY DON'T ASK QUESTIONS, AND DECIDE IN A MINUTE.

GOT ANY TOOT-TOOT, HON?

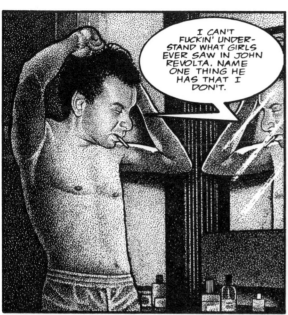

I CAN'T FUCKIN' UNDERSTAND WHAT GIRLS EVER SAW IN JOHN REVOLTA. NAME ONE THING HE HAS THAT I DON'T.

WEEKS LATER A CASANOVA GIRL CALLED WHOM MARNIN COULD FINALLY RELATE TO.

REMEMBER WHEN SHEMP GOES: "SAY, MOE, DOES MARSHMALLOWS HAVE PITS?" THAT LINE WAS ACTUALLY IN TWO EPISODES.

THAT SATURDAY, MARNIN DROVE AN HOUR TO RONKONKOMA. HIS HOPES AND DREAMS WERE SET ON A KNOCKOUT, AS PROMISED.

THE DOOR OPENED AND HIS HEART SANK.

HI. I DESIGNED THIS DRESS. SEXY, HUH?

THE NEXT THREE HOURS OF MY LIFE SACRIFICED TO FEMALE DOGDOM. IF I WASN'T SUCH A NICE GUY, I'D TAKE OFF....

THE WAITRESS AT THE BISTRO WAS THE MOST BEAUTIFUL WOMAN MARNIN HAD SEEN ALL YEAR.

I'LL HAVE ANOTHER SUNDAE. UMMM, YUMMY.

SHIT, SHE ALREADY PACKED HER FACE WITH TWO... AND AT FIVE BUCKS A POP.

MARNIN'S DATE WAS A 32-YEAR-OLD "FASHION DESIGNER" STILL LIVING WITH MOMMY AND DADDY.

LATELY, I'VE BEEN WAKING UP LATE.

HOW LATE?

TEN O'CLOCK.

YOU CALL THAT LATE? GUESS WHEN I ARISE?

WHEN?

FIVE.

WOW. I COULD NEVER GET UP THAT EARLY. FIVE A.M., THAT'S COMMENDABLE.

NO, FIVE IN THE AFTER-NOON.

OH...

UGGG. YUM YUM. BRRAPP, AHHH, YUMMY, UGGG. I HAVE ORGASMS OVER SUNDAES!

WARNING, WARNING. BRAIN DAMAGE, STAY AWAY!

GOSH, GEE... TIME TO GET OUT OF HERE.

MARNIN'S NEXT CASANOVA EVENING WAS MUCH THE SAME.

WHAT A SWEET COUPLE!

SHIT!

REELING FROM SEVERAL DISASTERS, MARNIN RETURNED.

WHAT YOU'VE SET ME UP WITH IS TOTALLY UNACCEPTABLE. I DON'T GIVE A DAMN IF YOU THINK I'M A MALE CHAUVINIST PIG.

IF YOU'RE LOOKING FOR A PERFECT 10 OUT OF PLAYBOY OR PENT-HOUSE, YOU'VE COME TO THE WRONG PLACE.

SINCE YOU'VE BROUGHT UP A 1-TO-10 SCALE, THE ONES YOU'VE SET ME UP WITH RATE BELOW 5. THEY WERE FEMALE DESPERADOES. LOOKS ARE VERY IMPORTANT TO ME. THE GIRL I BROKE UP WITH WAS A 7½. WITH-OUT AN INITIAL PHYSICAL AT-TRACTION, THERE IS NO CHANCE. I DON'T CARE IF SHE'S OTHERWISE THE GREATEST WOMAN IN THE WORLD.

GIVE US ONE MORE CHANCE. I HAVE JUST THE GIRL FOR YOU.... OF COURSE, WE'LL NEED THE BALANCE OF THE FEE.

GROWN MEN WHO SELL COMIC BOOKS?! THEY ARE...

COMIC SHOP CLERKS OF NORTH AMERICA

BENNY

MORDECAI

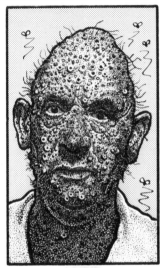

STEVE

MIKEY

RUSS

JEFF & JIFFY

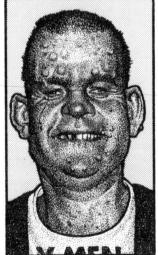

DOGDERBEK

"CHAPPY"

"Just then it hit me...*EVERYBODY* in the joint had Acromegaly."

DAMES MAKE THE MAN

ON HIS OWN, ARTEMUS THE PHLEGMY, HACKING ELEVATOR MAN, COULDN'T COMMAND THE ATTENTION OF A ROACH

Script: Josh Alan Friedman

BUT MATCH HIM UP WITH A HIGH-FALOOTIN' GOLDDIGGER AT THE COPA·· EVERYONE WOULD THINK HE MUST BE THE CAT'S PAJAMAS.

MARCUS BOJOHNSON, JR., NIGHT CUSTODIAN AT 1519 BROADWAY, COULDN'T GET SPIT UPON.

TH MOP IS MY MISTRESS.

SLAP A TOP MODEL ON HIS ARM, WITH TWO TICKETS TO THE APOLLO--PEOPLE MIGHT MISTAKE HIM FOR THE KING OF ETHIOPIA.

YOU'RE MY JANITORIAL DREAM.

ROTO-ROOTER MAN, GUS, SMELT SO BAD HOUSEWIVES RAN. BUT FOLKS WERE INTRIGUED WHEN HE BEGAN SHOWING UP ON CALLS BETWIXT A DUET OF HOT TAMALES.

AN' AWAY GO TROUBLES DOWN TH' DRAIN.

LIKEWISE, THE SECRETARIAL POOL DOWN AT THE OFFICE LOOKED AT JOE LIKE HE WAS SHIT. TILL THE DAY HE STROLLED IN WITH FIFI ON HIS ARM.

ON THE OTHER HAND, EVEN THE SHARPEST RACONTEUR MIGHT LOSE STATURE IF HE WERE SEEN IN THE WRONG COMPANY.

SO REMEMBER, GENT, WHEREVER YOU GO: DAMES MAKE THE MAN!

END

STOOGE WOMEN

HELEN

WHAT KIND OF GUY WAS HE? YOU GOT TO FIGURE THAT ANY GUY THAT MAKES A LIVING SMACKING HIS BROTHER AND ANOTHER GUY AROUND IS GONNA BRING A LITTLE OF THAT HOME ...

HE FINALLY GAVE JERRY A STROKE, BEATING ON HIM SO MUCH. DIDN'T STOP HIM AT ALL. HE JUST BROUGHT IN ANOTHER BROTHER TO SMACK AROUND. HE WAS NO PICNIC TO LIVE WITH.

MABEL

THE HOWARD BROTHERS WERE VERY CLOSE, BUT THEY HAD THAT FAMILY FRICTION, ESPECIALLY AFTER JERRY DIED. AFTER THAT, THE OTHER TWO WERE ALWAYS FIGHTING. MY LARRY HAD TO PLAY THE PEACE MAKER OFFSTAGE, TOO, AT LEAST UNTIL THE JOE'S CAME ALONG. AND BY THEN, IT WAS JUST A MONEY MAKING OPERATION AND EVERYONE WAS TOO OLD TO FIGHT. MY LARRY WAS A ROCK.

GERTRUDE

DON'T BELIEVE THAT CRAP ABOUT THEM NOT GETTING ALONG. THEY WERE BROTHERS, THEY WERE MAKING GOOD MONEY. LARRY WAS A PAIN IN THE ASS, ALWAYS TRYING TO GET A FIDDLE TUNE IN THE PICTURES. BUT MY HUSBAND GOT ALONG WITH EVERYBODY. HE FELT BAD ABOUT JERRY, BUT THE SHOW MUST GO ON. SO HE JUMPED AT THE CHANCE TO REPLACE HIM. I LOVED HIM. HIS BREATH SMELLED LIKE HE BRUSHED HIS TEETH WITH SHIT, BUT I LOVED HIM.

ELAINE

JERRY CHANGED WIVES THE WAY SOME MEN CHANGED SHIRTS. I WAS JUST ONE OF MANY, BUT I'LL LOVE HIM TILL THE DAY I DIE. HE RESENTED HIS BROTHER FOR MAKING HIM SHAVE HIS HEAD FOR THE ACT, BUT I THINK IT'S WRONG TO BLAME HIM FOR JERRY'S DEATH. JERRY KNEW THE PHYSICAL ABUSE WAS JUST PART OF THE JOB.

HE WAS INSECURE BECAUSE OF HIS WEIGHT. I THINK HE COMPENSATED BECAUSE OF THAT. HE WAS VERY LOVING IN THE BEDROOM. THE ONLY ODD THING WAS-- AT THE MOMENT OF CLIMAX, HE'D THROW HIS HEAD BACK AND GO "WOO! WOO! WOO!" I THINK THAT'S WHERE HE GOT IT FOR THE ACT. HE WAS REAL GOOD IN THE GARDEN, TOO.

END

HOLLYWOOD'S WILDEST LOVE DUOS

LEADING OFF WITH A BANG, PERHAPS HOLLYWOOD'S MOST NAUSEATING COUPLE. ONE CAN ONLY SHUDDER AT THE THOUGHT OF INTIMACY BETWEEN ERNEST BORGNINE AND ETHEL MERMAN.

DURING HOLLYWOOD'S HEYDAY, LEADING MAN ERROL FLYNN AND SISSY CHARACTER ACTOR FRANKLIN PANGBORN WERE A POPULAR PARTY COUPLE.

SWEETHEART, PERHAPS YOU CAN CARRY **ME** AROUND FOR A WHILE NOW, HMM ?

THE STRANGE AFFAIR BETWEEN ACROMEGALY-AFFLICTED ACTOR RONDO HATTON AND JOAN CRAWFORD WAS CUT SHORT BY HATTON'S UNTIMELY DEATH.

TELL ME SOMETHING, RONDO... THIS DISEASE OF YOURS... DOES IT ENLARGE ANY **OTHER** PARTS OF THE BODY ?

HEAVYWEIGHT CHAMP JOE LOUIS'S AFFAIR WITH NORWEGIAN SKATER-ACTRESS SONJA HENIE IS MYSTIFYING TO THIS DAY.

KNOCK 'IM OUT AND I'LL SUCK "LI'L BROWN BOMBER" LATER!

BETWEEN MARRIAGES, MARILYN MONROE ENJOYED A BRIEF LIAISON WITH SWEDISH WRESTLER-ACTOR-ZOMBIE TOR JOHNSON.

WHAT JOE DIMAGGIO AND ARTHUR MILLER GOT THAT TOR DON'T GOT ?

THE WACKIEST LOVE MATCH, THOUGH, HAS TO HAVE BEEN THE ROMANCE SHARED BY TALLULAH BANKHEAD AND HATTIE McDANIEL. THE MIND BOGGLES....

DAHLING, TELL ME IT WILL ALWAYS BE LIKE THIS !

END

ENTER-TAINMENT FREAK

IN JUNE OF 1961, DAVE AND MIRIAM GROUSE SPEND THEIR SPRING GETAWAY WEEKEND IN THE BORSCHT BELT.

I CAME TO BE ENTERTAINED.

OH, SHUT UP.

IT WAS ENTERTAINMENT THEY WANTED, AND ENTERTAINMENT THEY GOT. THAT NIGHT, DAVE BROKE IN HIS FINEST BAGGY PANTS TO THE JUNGLE RHYTHMS OF CUGAT.

FROM THERE, THE FUN COUPLE LAND A FRONT-TABLE REZ FOR THE DINNER SHOW AT GROSSINGER'S.

THE FEWD IS TENDER.

JUST SHUT YOUR MOUTH.

Script: Josh Alan Friedman

STUFFED TO THE GILLS, ENGAGED IN THE DIGESTIVE PROCESS, DAVE'S HAMMY BUTTOCKS SINK COMFORTABLY INTO HIS SEAT. THE TENSION MOUNTS.

BRING ME MY ENTERTAINMENT. BOY, DO I NEED SOME.

EUREKA, THE GROUSES ARE IN LUCK! OPENING THE SHOW ARE SANDLER & YOUNG, ROMANTIC SONG STYLISTS.

TO YOUR ENTERTAINMENT.

THE ENTERTAINMENT-STARVED COUPLE SOAK UP THE GLAMOUR.

A PRETTY GIRL...

AH, THAT'S GOOD ENTERTAINMENT.

BUT THEN, THE ENTERTAINMENT GOES PERHAPS A TAD TOO FAR.

IS LIKE A MELODY...

PPFFFFT

DAVE'S LOVELY WIFE, MIRIAM, CUTS THE EVENING SHORT.

NO MORE ENTERTAINMENT MISTER, YOUR NIGHT IS OVER.

BUT I NEED MY ENTERTAINMENT.

END

But today... I count on my friends for a roof over my head. My life has been destroyed by rotten romances and friendships turned sour. Drugs have affected me personally and every cent I've earned has disappeared. And now-- most terrifying of all-- I'm facing the possibility I'll be sent to prison.

But I haven't given up! I want everyone who thinks they've hit rock bottom to know that you CAN come back. You'll see the name "Joey Heatherton" in lights again-- and a star on my dressing-room door. I'm telling my story as a warning. If I can save one person from being destroyed like I've been, it will be worth revealing the humiliating facts behind my downfall.

I started in show business at age 10, the daughter of bandleader Ray Heatherton. He was later known on TV as--you guessed it, kids--"The Merry Mailman."

He met my mom when they starred in "Babes in Arms" on Broadway in 1937. Seven years later, I practically fell out of the crib into show biz.

I studied ballet under Balanchine. The dancing Blackburn twins occasionally put me in their hot night-club act at the Pierre.

THEN RICHARD RODGERS CHOSE ME FOR A SMALL BROADWAY REPLACEMENT ROLE -- AS A POSTULANT NUN -- AT AGE 14, IN "THE SOUND OF MUSIC."

ARE YOU KIDDING? SHE WAS A STUNNING CHILD. SHE DIDN'T HAVE THAT EXTRA SOPHISTICATION SHE HAS NOW, BUT SHE WAS, EVEN THEN, AWFULLY ATTRACTIVE.

JOSH LOGAN SIGNED ME TO A LEAD IN THE SHORT-LIVED "THERE WAS A LITTLE GIRL," ON BROADWAY WITH JANE FONDA.

SHE WAS BRIGHT AS A BUTTON AND SHE PROJECTED PRECISELY THE QUALITY WE NEEDED -- THAT OF A PERT TEENAGER WHO WAS VERY ADVANCED IN HER KNOWLEDGE OF MEN.

AT 15, I WAS OFFERED THE LEAD IN "LOLITA," BUT MY WIZENED FATHER PUT HIS FOOT DOWN.

PLEASE, DADDY, PLEASE!

NO! SUCH A CHARACTERIZATION WOULD BE PROFESSIONAL SUICIDE FOR ANY YOUNG ACTRESS.

MY SEASON ON *PERRY COMO* WAS GOING FINE -- UNTIL ALL THIS STUPID MAIL STREAMED IN FROM THE BIBLE BELT. THEY COMPLAINED ABOUT THIS "LOLITA THING." FER CHRIS SAKE, I LED A PERFECT VIRGINAL EXISTENCE, BUT THEY CALLED ME A LITTLE SEX TRAP.

CATCH A FALLING STAR AND PUT IT IN *YOUR* POCKET...

ANYHOW, TV PARTS ROLLED IN. *THE NURSES, THE VIRGINIAN, MR. NOVAK,* YOU NAME IT. I WAS HEADED FOR THE TIPPY TIPPY TOP, WITH A TEAM OF AGENTS AND COACHES. I SIGNED A 7-YEAR MOVIE CONTRACT IN '63. COULD YOU BELIEVE THE IDIOTS WANTED TO CHANGE MY NAME, CLAIMING I WASN'T "YET KNOWN."

PERHAPS SOMETHING MORE FEMININE -- LIKE "JOY"?

FORGET IT, PAL. I'D RATHER BE CALLED "ARPÈGE."

DICK ASTOR, MY PERSONAL MANAGER, MOLDED MY CAREER. HE WOULDN'T TAKE A ROLE UNLESS IT WAS ABSOLUTELY RIGHT. LISTEN, CHARLIE. HE PICKED 'EM, NOT ME.

TWILIGHT OF HONOR, MY DEBUT. MY DISTURBING "SLUT DANCE" MADE MEN MAD WITH DESIRE.

EEEWWWW!

MY **BLOOD RUNS COLD.** I CO-STARRED WITH TROY DONAHUE. CAN'T BEAT THAT.

OH, DADDY, I WISH WE COULD START ALL OVER AGAIN AND UNDO EVERYTHING.

WHERE LOVE HAS GONE. WE TURNED DOWN KUBRICK FOR **LOLITA,** BUT HERE I AM IN MY THIRD TURKEY, PLAYING A 14-YEAR-OLD MURDERESS WHO KILLS HER MOTHER'S LOVER.

THERE WAS NO LOGIC TO CONTINUE PLAYING MURDERERS AND PREGNANT UNWED TEENAGERS AND ALL THESE LITTLE... PSYCHOS. YOU NEVER SAW DEBBIE REYNOLDS PLAYING SOME LITTLE UNWED CLYDE. I COULD CRY, BUT I COULD ALSO LAUGH. I WANTED TO SMILE, TO GLOW... TO **ACT.** THE ONLY WAY THE PUBLIC COULD LOVE ME WAS IF I WAS GIVEN A SYMPATHETIC PART.

MY "FAME TEAM" WORKED THE PRESS.

JOEY DOESN'T SMOKE OR DRINK. EXEMPLARY LIVING HABITS.

SUSAN SEATON, VOICE COACH

STILL LIVES AT HOME IN ROCK-VILLE CENTER WITH HER PARENTS.

LAWRENCE LEVY, BUSINESS MGR.

A DISCIPLINED PRO WHO REHEARSES LONG HOURS.

DAVENIE, JOEY'S MOM

JOEY TAKES COMMUNION REGULARLY. HER FRIENDS ARE STILL THE GIRLS SHE WENT TO ST. AGNES WITH; SHE DOESN'T DATE ANYONE STEADILY.

MARY TARCAI, DRAMA COACH

DICK ASTOR SET FIRM SIGHTS ON A SPECIFIC TARGET, TURNING DOWN ALL FILM OFFERS FOR MY HOT LITTLE BOD.

IT WILL HAVE TO BE A TECHNICOLOR MOVIE, A COMEDY ROLE; SOMEWHAT DIZZY, KOOKY, CONTEMPORARY. AND IT WILL BE A ROLE IN WHICH SHE SINGS AND DANCES.

ALAS, IT WAS A ROLE WHICH NEVER CAME. IF ONLY I COULD'VE LANDED SOME OF ANN-MARGRET'S OR HALEY MILLS' KOOKIE PARTS. BUT I DANCED ON T.V. WITH A VENGEANCE. MY BIG CONTROVERSY CAME DURING **HULLABALLOO** WHEN I INTRODUCED A NUMBER COMBINING ALL THE NEW TEEN DANCES.

GUHRRR-OOVY.

BOSTON

WATUSI

MONKEY

PONY

JERK

SWIM

MOUSE

NBC SWITCHBOARDS LIT UP WITH THOUSANDS OF OUTRAGED CALLS. NEWSPAPERS SAID "MISS HEATHERTON'S FRUG IS THE MOST TORRID, UNINHIBITED, BONELESS EXHIBITION EVER SEEN ON T.V."

IF THIS DANCE IS ANY INDICATION, OUR TEENAGERS ARE GOING TO HECK IN A HANDBASKET.

LISTEN, CHARLIE, IF YOU WALKED INTO ANY DISCOTHEQUE, 16-YEAR-OLDS WERE DOING SEXIER DANCES. BUT THE CAMERAMAN FOCUSED RIGHT ON MY DERRIÈRE. IT WAS BANNED DUE TO PUBLIC PROTEST.

DO YOU ENJOY BEING A SEX-POT?

ARE YOU KIDDING? WHATEVER MAKES YOU THINK I'M A SEXPOT? I'M A SERIOUS ACTRESS... AND DANCER... AND SINGER. I DON'T TRY TO BE SEXY. THAT WOULD BE SOOO RIDICULOUS.

AFTER *HULLABALOO* I WAS A BONA FIDE SEX SYMBOL, AND COULDN'T SHAKE IT. MY PERSONAL APPEARANCES SHOT UP TO 5 GRAND PER.

"MISS HIGH VOLTAGE"

"NEW STAR OF THE YEAR"

"QUEEN OF ARTISTS AND MODELS BALL, 1966"

LOOK OUT, WORLD, HERE COMES JOEY. THEY DOUBLE-BOOKED ME ON *I SPY, HOLLYWOOD PALACE, ANDY WILLIAMS,* FRANK SINATRA, JR. AND I ENTERTAINED AMERICA ON THE PREMIERE "DEAN MARTIN GOLDDIGGERS" VARIETY SHOW.

I'M JUST A LITTLE GIRL WHO'S LOOKING FOR A LITTLE BOY...

LOOK MAGAZINE COINED MY HAIRDO "THE JOEY--A CORN-SILK YELLOW CUT, SOMEWHERE BETWEEN THE BEATLES AND DENNIS THE MENACE." BUT THE PRESS KEPT HOUNDING ME ON ONE SUBJECT, AND IT WAS KILLING MY ACTING CAREER.

THAT SEX THING. THE LAST OFFER WAS $12,000 IF SHE'D POSE ONCE FOR *PLAYBOY.* SOME GIRLS, THEY NEED TO, BUT NOT JOEY. SHE AIN'T GONNA DO THAT URSULA ANDRESS BIT. SHE'S GOT A LOT GOING AND DON'T NEED TO GO NAKED TO PROVE IT.

JACK TIRMAN, PUBLICIST.

I TOLD THOSE PESTS TO BUG OFF. I HAD HIGHER GOALS. MY VIETNAM TRIPS COST ME THOUSANDS IN BOOKINGS. THE M.P.'S HADDA HOLD 'EM BACK.

GO, BABY, GO!

WITH MY BEE-STUNG POUTY LIPS, I WAS TAKING OVER THE WORLD. MY ACCOUNTANT TOLD ME I OWNED OFFICE BUILDINGS, A RESTAURANT, A $2 MILLION MANHATTAN PENTHOUSE, AND A MANSION IN L.A.

WHAT COULD BE MORE WHOLESOME THAN MARRYING LANCE RENTZEL OF THE DALLAS COWBOYS. WE WERE BOTH FROM PEDIGREED FAMILIES. I JUMPED OUT OF MY SKIN WHENEVER LANCE CAUGHT A PASS. WE HAD A STORYBOOK WEDDING AT ST. PAT'S CATHEDRAL, APRIL 12, 1969.

LANCE WAS AN AMERICAN GOD. HIS NAME SOUNDED MORE LIKE A MACHINE THAN A MAN. BUT THEN SOMETHING AWFUL HAPPENED THAT TURNED MY LIFE UPSIDE DOWN.

HI, WANNA PLAY WITH BALDY THE CLOWN?

LANCE RENTZEL CHARGED 2ND TIME AS CHILD MOLESTER

I STUCK BY HIM THROUGH THE HUMILIATING TRIALS AND HEADLINES, BUT FINALLY HAD TO DIVORCE HIM. LANCE CONFESSED THE ONLY REASON HE MARRIED ME WAS FOR MY SHOW-BIZ CONNECTIONS TO BECOME A STAR HIMSELF.

MY LIFE WAS SHATTERED... UNTIL A MARVELOUS MAN CAME TO MY RESCUE. RICHARD BURTON. I FLEW TO HUNGARY FOR MY COMEBACK ROLE IN *BLUEBEARD*. I COULD NO LONGER AVOID THE CALL OF NUDITY -- THE WORLD WANTED MY NAY-NAYS EXPOSED. THE NUDITY WAS ESSENTIAL TO THE PLOT, I GUESS. FUNNY, WHEN YOU FISH 'EM OUT, IT'S NOT THE CHARACTER BEING EXPOSED, IT'S THE ACTRESS.

I WAS SUPPOSED TO BE LOOKING INTO HIS EYES AS I KISSED HIM. ELIZABETH STAYED SO CLOSE TO THE CAMERA, I LOOKED INTO HER EYES INSTEAD. SHE WAS VERY NICE AND SMILED.

FEAST YOUR EYES!

I WAS STILL A WOMAN HURTING OVER A BROKEN MARRIAGE. RICHARD FLIRTED WITH ME, BUILT MY CONFIDENCE BACK UP. I RETURNED TO THE U.S. OF A. BRASH AND COCKY AS EVER!

Variety

"JOEY HEATHERTON IS SO LEGGY, LOVELY AND THAT WE'VE DECIDED SHE MAY BE THE GREATEST BLONDE OF OUR DAY... TOMORROW'S SUPER-STAR!"

Earl Wilson ~ NY Post

THE 40s GAVE US GARLAND THE 50s INTRODUCED US TO MONROE THE 60's PRODUCED STREISAND. NOW, GET READY FOR THE 70s...THE ERA OF HEATHERTON!

James Bacon LA Herald Examiner

NOW AT CAESARS PALACE

THE MOVIES TREATED ME LIKE A HAS-BEEN/ NEVER-WILL-BE. WELL, SCREW HOLLYWOOD, CHARLIE. MY CLUB DRAW WAS STELLAR-- THEY *ALL* CAME TO SEE JOEY. I GOT $1.5 MILLION FROM THE SAHARA IN VEGAS, AND A QUARTER-MIL FOR A POSTER.

I WANNA BE LOVED BY YOU, JUST YOU AND NOBODY ELSE BUT YOU...

I WAS A DECADE AHEAD OF FONDA WITH MY AEROBIC DANCE WORKOUTS, WHICH I DEMONSTRATED AS CO-HOST FOR A WEEK ON MIKE DOUGLAS.

IF *I* TRIED THAT, I'D FART LIKE A BABOON.

YOU LADIES SHOULD TRY THIS.

MY SERTA PERFECT SLEEPER CAMPAIGN SOLD THOUSANDS OF MATTRESSES. WHAT MAN DIDN'T DREAM OF JOEY IN HIS BED?

PRRRR

I'LL BUY IT!

THE JOEY IMAGE BOOSTED BUSINESS FOR OTB AND A NATIONAL HARDWARE CHAIN. I CONQUERED THE TITLE ROLE OF *HAPPY HOOKER GOES TO WASHINGTON*, BUT SOME CRITIC SAID, "ACTING AND JOEY HEATHERTON HAVE APPARENTLY NEVER BEEN INTRODUCED." UGGGHHH! ...THEN I MET JERRY FISHER ...A DRUMMER WHO'D WORKED WITH LIZA. WE BECAME LOVERS. I LET HIM BECOME MY ROAD MANAGER.

WE GOT PLANS, *BIG* PLANS, FOR JOEY.

I GAVE HIM *TOO MUCH* POWER, AND EVERYONE IN SHOW BUSINESS KNEW IT.

I'D HEARD STORIES ABOUT THIS "BOYFRIEND." THAT MAN WAS A BIG DRAIN ON HER. A MONSTER. I LOATHE HIM.

JERRY WAS DOING A LOUSY JOB MANAGING ME. WE LOST A LOT OF DEALS. CLUBS BEGAN TO ASSOCIATE MY NAME WITH BROKEN PROMISES-- AND THAT SPELLS THE END OF ANY PERFORMER'S CAREER. I STARTED USING 'SCRIPT DRUGS, POPPING 'LUDES.

WHA'D I DO?

MARTY'S SUPPER CLUB TERMINATED MY ENGAGEMENT, CLAIMING I ACTED "LEWD" ONSTAGE. I MEAN, WHAT'S WRONG WITH A LITTLE LEG AND CLEAVAGE...?

LAWSUITS, LAWSUITS, LAWSUITS. I HAD 'EM FROM THE I.R.S., GURNEY'S INN, AND A NEIGHBOR AT MY EAST 57th ST. PENTHOUSE. MY FINANCIAL PROBLEMS WENT HAYWIRE. BUT THE PASSPORT OFFICE TOOK THE CAKE. I ONLY HAD $100 BILLS, AND WAS TOLD TO COME BACK WITH $35 AND THE REQUIRED PHOTOS. I WAS ARRAIGNED FOR DISORDERLY CONDUCT.

LISTEN, CHARLIE, I'VE GOT A GODDAMN PLANE TO CATCH

I BECAME FRANTIC, ANOREXIC -- THE STRESS OF SEEING EVERYTHING I'D WORKED FOR DESTROYED WAS KILLING ME. I STOPPED EATING AND SLEEPING. ONE DAY A KNOCK CAME AT MY DOOR -- MEN RUSHED IN AND HANDCUFFED ME, THEN STUCK A HYPO IN MY ARM.

I AWOKE IN A PSYCHIATRIC HOSPITAL. FRIENDS AND FAMILY HAD ME COMMITTED! FOR 20 DAYS, I LIVED IN A CLOSET-SIZED CUBICLE. IT WAS WORSE THAN MY WORST NIGHTMARE.

WHEN I WAS RELEASED, I CAME AFTER JERRY FOR RUINING MY CAREER. HE BLAMED IT ON DRUGS. I GUESS I WENT INTO A RAGE. THE POLICE SAID I SLASHED HIS PHONE WIRES, THEN CORNERED THE BASTARD.

THEY SAY I ALLEGEDLY CUT HIM UP A LITTLE. THE ARRESTING COPS DIDN'T BELIEVE I WAS *THE* SEX GODDESS, JOEY HEATHERTON -- SO I DARED 'EM, JUST LOOK IN MY POCKETBOOK FOR PROOF...OOOPS. THEY FOUND MY COKE STASH.

G'WAN, CHARLIE, SEE FOR YERSELF.

NYAAAAA

THE **TOP** SHOCK SHOW OF **ALL** TIME

SPINE·CHILLING!

Weird!

Shocking!

ZACHERLEY
THE COOL GHOUL

SUPERSCOPE

GUARANTEED TO FRIGHTEN

© D.F.

HE'S BACK!

Thrills!

FOR THE FIRST TIME!

Terror!

ALL-NEW NIGHTMARE of FEAR and HORROR

LON CHANEY JR.

THE SCARY GUY

AMERICAN INTERNATIONAL PICTURES

© D.F.

SHE'S HOT MULE BAIT!

SEE!

The Most Delightful Character You've Ever Known!

MONOGRAM
presents

SEE!

ALL NEW THRILLS!

FREAK SHOW GIRL!

AMAZING!
EXPLOSIVE!
TERRIFYING!

© D.F.

starring "THE MULE-FACED WOMAN"

COLOR BY DE LUXE   A MONOGRAM PICTURE

MR. SPOOKY IS BACK!

NOW!

WE AIM TO SPOOK!

HOW-CO

© D.F.

Terrifying!...
Destructive!

starring LUGOSI • JOHNSON

BELA LUGOSI'S SCARIEST ROLE

THE PRESSURE OF BEING A MATINEE IDOL IN 1918, ADORED BY HUNGARIAN CHICKS, DREW HIM CLOSER TO NICOTINE.

HOLLYWOOD STARDOM WAS SWEET, BUT AN INABILITY TO GRAB BIGGER ROLES BY THE BALLS KEPT HIS CAREER IN CHECK. KARLOFF CONTINUALLY OVERSHADOWED THE HUNGARIAN, EVEN IN HIS SECOND-GREATEST ROLE.

BY THE FORTIES BELA'S PERSONA MADE HIM THE MOST TYPECAST ACTOR IN HOLLYWOOD.

THESE YOUNG PEOPLE TODAY.

LUGOSI SCORNED THE HORROR FILM, BUT SLOWLY RESIGNED HIMSELF TO THE FACT THAT HE HAD BEEN CONDEMNED TO A LIFETIME OF DYING ON THE SCREEN.

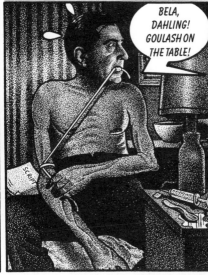

BELA, DAHLING! GOULASH ON THE TABLE!

HE BECAME THE FIRST RECIPIENT OF SHOW-BIZ PAYOLA, AS WE KNOW IT TODAY.

MORPHINE

BY THE EARLY FIFTIES, THE GREAT ROMANTIC ACTOR HAD HIT BOTTOM, RECITING THE BRAIN-TWISTING DIALOGUE OF AUTEUR ED WOOD, JR. IT WAS ALL HE COULD GET.

PULL THE STRING! DANCE TO THAT WHICH ONE IS CREATED FOR. WHY DOES THE BIG GREEN DRAGON SIT AT YOUR DOORSTEP? HE EATS LITTLE BOYS...PUPPY DOGS' TAILS AND BIG FAT SNAILS!

AT THE BROWN DERBY, EVEN HIS ACTING CHUMS WERE SOMEWHAT AGHAST AT BELA'S APPEARANCE WITHOUT MAKEUP.

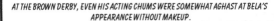

GOOD EVENING, MY FRIENDS.

BY 1955, BELA HAD, ALAS, PROVEN HIMSELF A POOR ADVERTISEMENT FOR DRUG REHABILITATION.

AT LEAST I'M STILL PERFORMINK.

END

BELA LUGOSI 1882-1956

The Heartbreak of Acromegaly

THE RONDO HATTON STORY

THE STRANGE CASE OF RONDO HATTON BEGINS ON THE PROMISING SIDE. YOUNG RONDO WAS TWICE VOTED MOST HANDSOME AND POPULAR FELLA IN HIS HIGH SCHOOL CLASS, AND LATER, AT THE UNIVERSITY OF FLORIDA, BECAME CAPTAIN OF THE FOOTBALL TEAM, THOUGH WEIGHING IN AT A SCANT 136.

HI, RONDO!

OH, RONDO!

HE'S A DREAM.

BUT COME WORLD WAR I, RONDO FOUND HIMSELF IN THE TRENCHES OF THE WESTERN FRONT, WHERE HE WAS EXPOSED TO CHEMICAL WARFARE...

...WHICH LED TO THE DISEASE ACROMEGALY (CHRONIC HYPERPITUITARISM), CHARACTERIZED BY PROGRESSIVE ENLARGEMENT OF THE HANDS, FEET, AND FACE, WHICH WOULD CURSE HIM FOR LIFE. RONDO LINGERED IN HOSPITALS FOR YEARS.

IN THE LATE THIRTIES, SEEKING A DRY CLIMATE, RONDO HEADED FOR SOUTHERN CALIFORNIA, WHERE HE FIRST FLIRTED WITH THE IDEA OF LETTING THE MOVIES EXPLOIT HIS WRETCHED FACE.

UNIVERSAL, SEEKING A NEW HORROR STAR, SAW GREAT POTENTIAL IN RONDO AND SIGNED HIM TO A LONG-TERM CONTRACT. HE WAS GIVEN A HUGE PUBLICITY BUILDUP AS "THE CREEPER."

RONDO MADE A SERIES OF SUCCESSFUL HORROR FILMS IN THE EARLY FORTIES, ALWAYS PLAYING A DERANGED DEFORMED MONSTER WHO KILLS PEOPLE WHEN THEY SCREAM AT HIS HORRIBLE FACE.

SADLY, RONDO'S NEWFOUND MOVIE STARDOM WAS FLEETING. HE DIED OF A HEART ATTACK IN 1946, LEAVING AUDIENCES TO THIS DAY STILL WONDERING ABOUT THE STRANGE CASE OF RONDO HATTON.

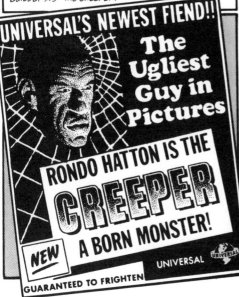

UGLY WHITE GUYS— THEY LIKE TELE- VISION

BUT WHAT ARE THEIR FAVORITE SHOWS?

"Lucha Libre"

"Beat the Clock"

"This Old House"

"Arsenio Hall"

"Pat Sajak"

"The New Monkees"

"The Simpsons"

"Flipper"

"Bowling for Dollars"

"Me and the Chimp"

"The Outer Limits"

"Bonanza"

"Batman"

"Me and the Chimp"

"Masterpiece Theatre"

Kitty Carlisle

"Petticoat Junction"

"Combat"

"The Bullwinkle Show"

"Mr. Ed"

"Tattle Tales"

"Ben Casey"

"Bridget Loves Bernie"

"The Jack Paar Show"

"The Cosby Show"

"Me and the Chimp"

"Amos 'n' Andy"

"F Troop"

"The Love Connection"

"Hee Haw"

Uncle Miltie

"The Brady Bunch"

MONDO DOBERMAN

AROUND THE WORLD WITH DUANE DOBERMAN. FIRST STOP: NEW YORK, N.Y.

IN CUBA, FUN AND FROLICKING FOR DOBERMAN DURING THE REVOLUTION.

AW, CASTRO, NO MORE SLOT MACHINES?!

DOBERMAN RENEWS HIS "FRIENDSHIP" WITH THE BEAUTEOUS MADAME DUBREUIL IN GAY PAREE.

OOH LA LA, DUANE...

NEXT STOP: HOLLYWOOD. DOBERMAN PAINTS THE TOWN RED WITH DEAR OLD CHUMS.

AW, HECK... TH' RED CARPET, JUST FOR ME?

THE "DANCE FOR DOBERMAN" IS PERFORMED BY THE SWADINKI TRIBESPEOPLE IN AFRICA.

HADDAYA LIKE DAT... NATIONAL GEOGRAPHIC COME TO LIFE!

ROUNDING OUT HIS JET-SETTING IN JAPAN, DOBERMAN DELIGHTS TO LOVELY GEISHA GIRLS.

NOW GIRLS... JUST DON'T DROP NO BOMBS ON MY HEAD.

BACK HOME, DOBERMAN PONDERS THIS VAST, WONDERFUL PLANET HE LIVES ON.

GEEZ, MAYBE I SHOULD GET A PEDICURE TOMORRA?

Home Sweet Home

END

BEAVER FACTS

"LEAVE IT TO BEAVER" HITS THE AIR IN LATE '57. IT WILL GO ON TO BECOME ONE OF THE MOST BELOVED SHOWS EVER.

IN 1963, THE CLEAVER CLAN WILL LEAVE THE AIR. THE SHOW'S PRODUCERS WILL NEXT GIVE US "THE MUNSTERS", ANOTHER FAMILY SITCOM. THE MUNSTER HOUSE IS LOCATED ON THE SAME BLOCK AS THE CLEAVER HOUSE AT UNIVERSAL STUDIOS.

IN THE LATE SIXTIES SHELLY WINTERS, GUESTING ON "THE TONIGHT SHOW", BLABS OF THE BEAVER'S MISFORTUNE IN VIETNAM. THIS SETS OFF RUMORS THAT WILL CONTINUE FOR YEARS.

WACKY HUMOR, HOME SPUN CHARM, AND SLICE OF LIFE SITUATIONS WILL KEEP THE CLEAVER FAMILY HIGH IN THE RATINGS FOR SEVEN YEARS.

AS THE SHOW MOVES INTO THE MID-SIXTIES, IT IS THE CHUNKHEAD* WALLY CLEAVER, WHO BEGINS TO SHINE AS THE STAR. AND THE GIRLS HAVE TAKEN NOTICE, TOO.

WELL, BEAVER. I GUESS ALL FATHERS DREAM OF THEIR LITTLE BOYS GROWING UP AND MARRYING THE BANKER'S DAUGHTER OR WINNING A SCHOLARSHIP. WE JUST DREAM THROUGH OUR CHILDREN.

YOU MEAN MR. RUTHERFORD EVEN DREAMS THROUGH LUMPY?

WALLY'S GORGEOUS!

OOOOOO WALLY CLEAVER!

SO CUTE!

SO FINE!

HE'S A DREAM-BOAT!

WALLY'S ADORABLE!

* PHRASE COINED BY MARNIN ROSENBERG OF GREAT NECK.

ANOTHER MUCH-HERALDED RUMOR CENTERED ON THE OBNOXIOUS FRIEND OF WALLY'S, EDDIE HASKELL, BECOMING PORN STAR JOHNNY WADD. (ACTUALLY, HE BECAME A L.A. COP.)

THE CLEAVERS AND FRIENDS REUNITED FOR A T.V. MOVIE AND SERIES IN THE MID-80'S MINUS WARD, WHO PASSED ON IN '82. BEAV AND WALLY EVEN POSED ON THE CORN FLAKES BOX. STAY TUNED!

GOOD MORNING, MRS. CLEAVER.

GOOD EVENING, MRS. CLEAVER.

Kellogg's CORN FLAKES

America's Favorite Cereal

END

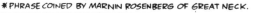

BILL CULLEN ON THE WILD SIDE

END

THE GREATEST STORY EVER

FLESH-CRAWLING ACTION!
Shocking!
Weird!

FUN!

Thrills!

HOWCO'S

HA, HA, HA

Andy Devine•Froggie CINEMASCOPE G

The most magnificent picture ever!

DEATH

LIFE

NEW THRILL WONDER
in 3-D!
THE SEASON'S MADDEST

VARIETY, SPICE AND EVERYTHING NICE © D.F.

OOH, JESUS!

JOE E. ROSS · STELLA STEVENS G

WACKY WORLD

MILTON BERLE, LEE HARVEY OSWALD,

JERRY LEWIS, ARTHUR BREMMER,

DAVID BERKOWITZ, RED BUTTONS,

EDWARD GEIN, BUDDY HACKETT,

MICKEY ROONEY, RICHARD SPECK,

CHARLES MANSON & BOB HOPE.

END

THE LORD PHONES LOU WASSERMAN, PRESIDENT OF MCA UNIVERSAL, WITH HIS ANNOUNCEMENT.

I SHALL PREPARE MY LIFE STORY FOR THE DELIGHT OF YOUR BANK ACCOUNT.

SIX WEEKS LATER THE LORD PUTS THE FINISHING TOUCHES ON HIS EPIC BIOGRAPHY.

I MUST FINISH *MY* BIO' BEFORE ABE VIGODA EVEN *BEGINS* HIS, OTHERWISE, A CONFLICT ENSUES.

A SUDDEN HYDROCEPHALIC BRAINSTORM HITS THE LORD AS HE SIFTS THROUGH THE 7,058 PAGE TOME.

I HAVE DECIDED THE ONLY MAN TO DO JUSTICE TO MY PORTRAYAL ON SCREEN IS BUDDY GRECO. I *MUST* HAVE HIM OR I WILL DIE.

THE LORD PHONES GROSSINGERS IN THE CATSKILLS IN SEARCH OF ENTERTAINER GRECO.

I'M SORRY SIR-- BUDDY GRECO HASN'T APPEARED HERE IN ABOUT EIGHT YEARS. THEODORE BIKEL IS OUR CURRENT ATTRACTION.

HAH! SURELY YOU JEST, MY GOOD MAN.

THE BEST-SELLING AUTHOR CAN ONLY SIT BACK AND ENJOY THE REWARDS OF HIS GREAT TALENTS, FAME, AND WEALTH.

TH' STINKIN' BASTIDS! I WANTED VIC DAMONE ALL ALONG.

END

THE LORD OF ELTINGVILLE HAS THE ANSWERS

NOT EVEN THE LORD OF ELTINGVILLE KNOWS ALL THE ANSWERS...

YET MANKIND HAS TAKEN IT UPON ITSELF TO SEEK OUT HIS KNOWLEDGE...

LEMME JUST UNBUTTON YOUR SHIRT AND GET A TASTE OF YOUR MANLINESS. OKAY??

BRING ME A PEZ DISPENSER WITH THE FACE OF MORTY GUNTY.

TELE-PHONE, LORD.

THE GOVERNMENT CAUGHT IN THE MIDDLE OF INTERNATIONAL INTRIGUE HAS NO ALTERNATIVE BUT TO ENGAGE THE LORD'S VALUABLE SERVICES.

BEGGING YOUR PARDON, LORD, BUT CAN YOU BE AT THE PENTAGON TONIGHT?

KIM NOVAK IS A FRIEND TO THE ANIMAL KINGDOM.

THE COUNTRY, SENSING THE WORST, BEGINS TO SPECULATE ON WHAT THIS MEETING IS ALL ABOUT.

ANY WORD?

WHAT'S GOING ON?

RUSSIANS?

SO NU?

DID YOU KNOW THAT MR. GREENJEANS DIED FOR YOUR SINS?

THE LORD MEETS FACE TO FACE WITH THE SECRETARY OF DEFENSE, THE ATTORNEY GENERAL, AND THE DIRECTOR OF THE C.I.A.

SIR, WE APPRE-CIATE YOU MEETING WITH US. CAN YOU INTERPRET THE SITUATION?

I'M IN THE MOOD FOR A ZAGNUT.

THE LORD GOES BEFORE THE MEDIA TO ANSWER THEIR QUESTIONS. THE EYES OF THE WORLD ARE UPON HIM.

FOR ONCE AND FOR ALL I DEMAND TO KNOW... IS JOHNNY MATHIS A NEGRO?

END

THE LORD OF ELTINGVILLE AND HIS PAL, FRANK SINATRA

THE LORD OF ELTINGVILLE AND SINGER FRANK SINATRA HAVE ENJOYED A DAZZLING FRIENDSHIP THAT HAS SPANNED NEARLY FOUR DECADES.

MEETING RECENTLY AT **JILLY'S** IN N.Y.C., THE TWO LEGENDS REFLECT ON THEIR **VERY GOOD YEARS** TOGETHER.

THEY RECALL THEIR LEGENDARY ALL-NIGHT GAMBLING SESSIONS AT THE SANDS, WHEN THE TWO WERE HEADLINING...

...THE FAMED NIGHTS ON THE STRIP, THE GENESIS OF THE LORD'S RAT PACK...,

INDEED, **OUR** FRIEND-SHIP HAS GROWN LIKE VINTAGE WINE FROM FINE OLD KEGS.

YOU'RE ONE HELL OF A GUY.

WE ALWAYS WIN BECAUSE WE LEAD CHARMED LIVES.

ONLY GINA LOLLOBRIGIDA CAN SATISFY MY CARNAL DESIRES.

YEAH, BUT DIG THE TABLE OF BIMBOS.

...THEIR WILD, RECKLESS, SWINGIN' ALL-NIGHT ORGIES HIGH ABOVE THE HOLLYWOOD HILLS.

YES, TRULY A FANTASTIC FRIENDSHIP BETWEEN TWO OF THE GREATS OF THE 20TH CENTURY.

SWEETHEART, **YOU** ARE MY ONE DESIRE, AN' I MEAN THAT SINCERELY.

DARLING, IN TH' WEE SMALL HOURS OF THE MORN-ING, DELIGHT ME WITH SOME FELLATIO.

♪ FRANKIE, WITH TH' LAUGHING FACE ♪

END

TOR JOHNSON MEETS THE LORD OF ELTINGVILLE ON A TRAIN

THE LORD OF ELTINGVILLE DELIGHTS IN THE COUNTRYSIDE FROM HIS PRIVATE TRAIN COMPARTMENT.

TOR JOHNSON SEARCHES IN VAIN FOR *HIS* PRIVATE TRAIN COMPARTMENT.

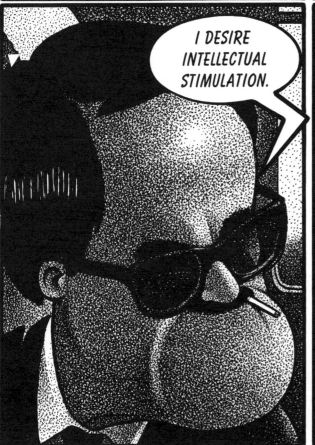

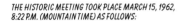

TOR JOHNSON IN NEW YORK

TOR JOHNSON'S 1963 NEW YORK VACATION INCLUDED A VISIT TO SLEAZY TIMES SQUARE. IT WAS THERE THAT THE FOLLOWING TRANSACTION TOOK PLACE.

WHILE CROSSING THE OLD MILLER BRIDGE, TOR PAUSES TO RELIEVE HIMSELF.

TOR MAKE NUMBER ONE.

UNBEKNOWNST TO TOR, A MEAN AND MISERABLE OLD BUM IS TRYING TO CATCH A FEW WINKS BENEATH THE BRIDGE.

SPLAT!

WHO'S RAININ' ON MY PARADE?!

WHO THE HELL DO YOU THINK YOU ARE?

TOR!

BONK!

NEXT TIME, TOR MAKE NUMBER TWO.

END

DICK CLARK MODELS ROCK HAIRSTYLES

DICK CLARK

ELVIS

LITTLE RICHARD

'64 BEATLES

JIMI HENDRIX

MIKE NESMITH

JERRY GARCIA

BOB MARLEY

SID VICIOUS

GRACE JONES

MICHAEL JACKSON

TINA TURNER

Dick Clark gives his *American Bandstand* replacement a few pointers.

On a search for new musical inspiration, David Byrne unexpectedly runs into Paul Simon.

Successful, important entertainer-educator-author Bill Cosby is never too busy to consider a financial opportunity.

Former comedian Dan Aykroyd chooses movie scripts for future roles.

Republican National Committee chairman, Lee Atwater, entertains some friends with a negro spiritual.

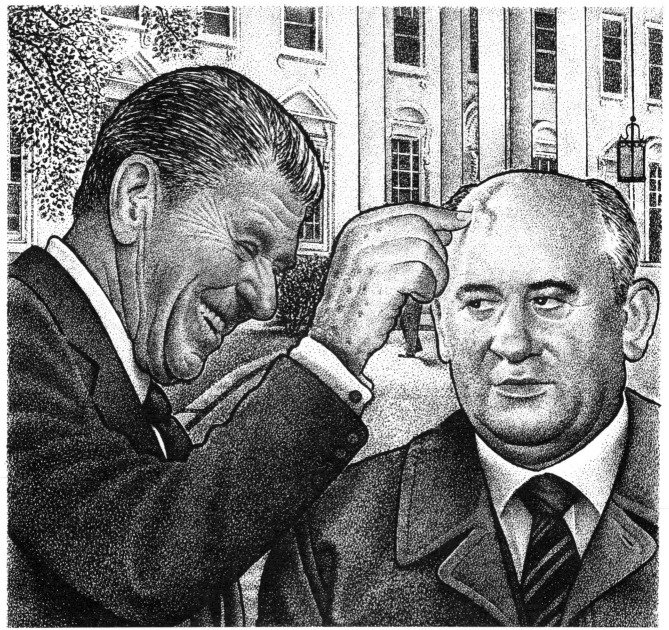

Ronald Reagan raises a new issue with General Secretary Gorbachev.

George Bush shares some humor with an appreciative golfing chum.

Vice President Dan Quayle and family enjoy some quality time together on a Sunday afternoon.

ALLITERATION

On a peaceful portion of a proud
population the atom bomb fell
Tall trees tormented by the
tempest twisted and toppled
Finned and feathered fauna fought
with frenzy then fell
Indigenous insects were
immediately inculcated with
their immense insecurity
Big buildings bulged and buckled
then burst and burned
Slimy serpents stealthily slid
beneath partially sunken stones
Man was marred and mutilated
Children were chopped and
charred
Woman was wantonly wasted
Gone from the face of a forlorn
world was man along with his
multitudinous achievements
And at long last...
Peace reigned the earth.

A poem by Leo Gorcey, from *Dead End Yells,
Wedding Bells, Cockle Shells, and Dizzy Spells.*
Vantage Press, New York, 1967. ©1967 Leo Gorcey.

GLOSSARY
GUIDE FOR THE PERPLEXED

Adams, Cindy (ad'ams sen'dē) N.Y. gossip columnist and society sycophant.

Atwater, Lee (at'wot-ər lē) Republican Party Chairman. Alleged lover of blues music.

Berkowitz, David (bĕrk'ō-witz dā'vid) "Son of Sam" serial killer in New York, late '70s.

Berle, Milton (bĕrl mil'tun) "Mr. Television" from 1948–1956. Hosted unsuccessful prime-time bowling series in '60s.

Bikel, Theodore (bə kel' thē'ō dôr) Monotonous, multi-lingual folk singer character actor. Appeared in original Broadway *Sound of Music*, and *My Fair Lady* on screen.

Blackburn Twins (blak'bĕrn twins) Nightclub entertainers. Ran first-class pizzeria on Long Island, N.Y. in '60s.

Bremmer, Arthur (brem'ĕr är'thĕr) Attempted assassin of Alabama Gov. George Wallace.

Buttons, Red (but'ens red) Oscar-winning comedian, and Florida real estate pitchman to senior citizens.

Chaney Jr., Lon (chän'ē joon'yər län) 1906–1973. Famed Hollywood horror, character actor, most remembered for *The Wolf Man* and *Of Mice and Men.*

Clark, Dick (klärk dik) Host of *American Bandstand* 1957–1988, and TV business tycoon of watered-down rock 'n' roll.

Cullen, Bill (kul'en bil) Durable TV game-show emcee since 1940s.

Damone, Vic (da'mōn vik) Crooner described by Sinatra as having "the best pipes in the biz."

Devine, Andy (di-vīn' ăn'dē) 1905–1977. High-pitched, hoarse-voiced character actor; Hollywood crony of Clark Gable. Hosted *Andy's Gang,* kids' variety show from 1955–1960.

Doberman, Duane (dō'bar-man dwān) Character portrayed by Maurice Gosfield on the *Bilko* TV series of the '50s. Women found him irresistible.

Donahue, Troy (don'ə-hū trōi) Untalented, blond leading man of dreck movie dramas, like *A Summer Place.*

Douglas, Mike (dug'las mīk) Bland, milquetoast talk show host from 1963 through mid-'70s. Former Midwestern radio singer.

Feldstein, Al (feld'stēn al) Editor, writer of most of the EC comics of the '50s and the second editor of *Mad.*

Fell, Norman (fel nôr'men) Played white-lipped, middle-aged divorced guys and landlords on TV and in Rat Pack-type films. Credits include *Ocean's II, Quick Before It Melts* and *The Graduate.*

Froggie (frâg'ē) Mischievous frog-gremlin on *Andy's Gang.*

Gein, Ed (gēn ed) 1906–1984. *Psycho* and *Texas Chainsaw Massacre* were vaguely based upon this Wisconsin killer.

Gorcey, Leo (gōr'sē le'ō) 1917–1967. Tough guy star of Dead End Kids, East Side Kids and Bowery Boys movie series. Died the same year his poem "Alliteration" was written.

Greco, Buddy (gre'cō bud'ė) Lounge-saloon singer, would-be toppler of, say, Steve Lawrence's throne.

Greenjeans, Mr. (grēn'jēns mis'tər) Sidekick of kiddie show host Captain Kangaroo.

Guccione, Bob (gü-chē-'ōn·ē bäb) Absurdly wealthy, imperfectly groomed founder of *Penthouse* magazine.

Gunty, Morty (gun'tē môr'tē) Obscure, amiable standup comic, peaked in '60s.

Hackett, Buddy (hak'it bud'ē) Annoying, un-funny comedian of film, T.V., and nightclubs.

Hall, Huntz (hâl huntz) Comedic co-star—sidekick of Leo Gorcey in the same series.

Henie, Sonja (hen'ē sōn'yà) 1916-1973. Swedish ice-skating champion who skated her way into B-movies of yore.

Henry, John (hen'rē jon) Subject of 19th century folk song based on steel-driving Negro of American railroad folklore, who beat the steam drill in a duel with his hammer. ("*Then he laid down his hammer and he died, Lord, Lord. . .*")

Jilly's (jil'ēs) Midtown New York restaurant owned by Sinatra bodyguard, Jilly Rizzo.

Johnson, Tor (jon'sen tòr) 1903–1971. The beloved giant Swede, who professionally wrestled for years before shaving his dome and achieving movie infamy in countless cheap horror films.

Logan, Josh (lō'gan josh) 1908–1988. Distinguished director of stage and screen, whose Broadway credits include *Mister Roberts* and *South Pacific*.

Lopez, Trini (lōpez trē'nē) Popular '60s singer who had danceable hits with "If I Had a Hammer" and "Lemon Tree".

McDaniel, Hattie (mac-dan'yel hat'ē) 1895–1952. Oscar-winning "Mammy" in *Gone With The Wind.*

Novak, Mr. (no'vak mis'ter) Dramatic NBC series (1963–1965) about idealistic young teacher.

Nurses, The (nērs'is the) Dramatic CBS series (1962–1964) set in hospital.

OTB (ō t b) Off Track Betting.

Pangborn, Franklin (pang'bôrn frank lin) 1894–1958. Golden Hollywood's ubiquitous swishy character actor of the '30s.

Ross, Joe E. (râs jō ē) 1917–1984. Wonderful comic actor who co-starred on the TV shows *Bilko* and *Car 54, Where Are You?*

Rutherford, Mr. (ruth'ərførd mis'tər) Lumpy's father in *Leave It To Beaver,* portrayed by Richard Deacon.

Sandler & Young (sand'lər and yung) Romantic, tuxedoed, champagne-toasting vocal duo marketed toward middle-aged housewives.

Southern, Terry (seth'ərn ter'ē) Perhaps America's most profoundly witty and original novelist/screenwriter (books include *Candy, The Magic Christian, Blue Movie;* screenplays include *Dr. Strangelove, Easy Rider, The Loved One*).

Speck, Richard (spek rich'ärd) Convicted of the murders of eight student nurses in 1966. Sentenced to 1,200 years in jail.

Stevens, Stella (ste'vens stel'ē) Blond, pouty actress. Co-star of *The Nutty Professor.*

Tamale (te-mä'lē) Hot Mexican dish wrapped in corn husk.

Vampira (vam'pīrə) Sultry, Finnish-born horror show hostess of late-nite Los Angeles TV during 1950s. Dated James Dean. Co-starred with Tor Johnson.

Vigoda, Abe (vig-ō'da āb) Boris Karloff-ish star of *Fish,* TV sitcom (1977–1978). Played Tessio in *The Godfather.* Career cursed by rumors of his death, which he continually fights to disprove.

Von Zell, Harry (von zel har'ē) George Burns' announcer on radio and TV.

Wood, Wally (wûd wâl'ē) 1927–1981. Troubled comics artist who specialized in science fiction.

Zacherley (zak'ər-lē) Legendary Kennedy-era late-nite horror movie host. Everyone's fave "cool-ghoul."

Zagnut (zag'nut) A candy bar.

Drew Friedman was born in New York City back in the fifties and for some reason remains there today. His comics and illustrations appear in publications such as *Raw*, *Weirdo*, *Blab*, *National Lampoon*, *The Village Voice*, and *Spy*, where he contributes a monthly feature. His first book, *Any Similarity to Persons Living or Dead is Purely Coincidental*, co-authored by Josh, continues to disturb mankind in extra printings. On other fronts, he illustrates the *News of the Weird* books and is co-creator of *Toxic High*, a new sticker series from Topps Gum. He lives happily with his wife Kathy and three cats.

Enslaved by two careers—writer and musician—Josh Alan Friedman continues his ascension as a Texas-based guitarist and songwriter. Performing nightly as ''Josh Alan,'' he remains on the cutting edge of Dallas' Deep Ellum music scene. On the book front, his romantic homage to New York, *Tales of Times Square*, is a first-hand non-fiction chronicle of the area's decline. Many of his short stories and articles have appeared in the nation's best and worst mags. A solo album is due to coincide with *Warts*, his third book.